Beast
Quest

Collect the special coins in this book.
You will earn one gold coin for
every chapter you read.

Once you have finished all the chapters,
find out what to do with your gold coins at
the

With special thanks to Tab Jones

For Adam Sefton

www.beastquest.co.uk

ORCHARD BOOKS

First published in Great Britain in 2018 by The Watts Publishing Group

1 3 5 7 9 10 8 6 4 2

Text © 2018 Beast Quest Limited.
Cover and inside illustrations by Steve Sims
© Beast Quest Limited 2018

Beast Quest is a registered trademark of Beast Quest Limited
Series created by Beast Quest Limited, London

The moral rights of the author and illustrator have been asserted.

A CIP catalogue record for this book is available from the British Library.

ISBN 978 1 40834 303 6

Printed and bound by CPI Group (IUK) Ltd, Croydon, CR0 4YY

The paper and board used in this book are made from wood from responsible sources

Orchard Books
An imprint of Hachette Children's Group
Part of The Watts Publishing Group Limited
Carmelite House, 50 Victoria Embankment, London EC4Y 0DZ

An Hachette UK Company
www.hachette.co.uk
www.hachettechildrens.co.uk

VeraK
THE STORM KING

BY ADAM BLADE

ORCHARD

GWILDOR

BAY OF GWILDOR

FISHING VILLAGE

NORTHERN MOUNTAINS

THE FOREST OF FEAR

THE WINDING RIVER

BAY OF AVANTIA

AVANTIA

CONTENTS

STORY ONE

THE SWORD IN THE SEA

Man the tiller, you toothless lump! That's right – take us to starboard!

I tell you, this crew of villains has bilge for brains! But at least they follow orders. They know they'd be food for sharks if they didn't. We make course from Makai to Gwildor. With the south winds blowing, we should reach the walls of their city within a day.

The crew think we're on a rescue mission to break their former captain out of the dungeon. And I admit, Sanpao might even be useful on this voyage, if he doesn't get too big for his boots. But the real prize is a bigger one by far, and raiding Gwildor's capital is just the first stage of the plan. For in the palace vault is a treasure that can unleash misery on the poor innocents of Gwildor and Avantia.

And the best part of all? No one can stop me...

Tighten the mizzen, you wretched scabs!
Your Captain, Ria of Makai

NEW FRIENDS, OLD ENEMIES

Practice sword in hand, Tom circled Amelia warily, watching her own wooden blade. Cheers rang out all around: "Come on, Tom!" and "Go, Amelia!" From the corner of his eye, Tom could see his mother, Freya, standing beside Queen Irina's throne at the front of the crowd, her silver armour blazing in the sun. As the

Mistress of the Beasts in Gwildor, Freya had been training Amelia since Tom's last visit. Beyond the courtyard wall and the elegant spires of Gwildor's palace, banners flapped in a sapphire-blue sky.

Amelia lunged, slashing downwards with her sword. *Clack!* Tom parried the blow, then jabbed up at Amelia's ribs. She leapt aside, returning Tom's strike with a two-handed swing. Tom ducked, hearing the blade whistle over his head, then slashed upwards. *SMACK!* His blade locked with Amelia's. They sprang apart, circling once more. Murmurs of approval ran through the gathered courtiers.

"Looks like you're getting slow in your old age, Tom!" Amelia said, her

blue eyes glinting.

"While you're as cocky as ever,"Tom answered. "I expected Mother to teach you some manners!" In fact, Tom felt amazed at how much Amelia had changed under Freya's tutelage. She'd grown taller, and lean muscles stood out on her sun-browned arms. Their swords met, sending a jolt of pain up Tom's shoulder as he blocked. He couldn't help being impressed by the speed and force of Amelia's blow.

Amelia swung again. Tom leapt out of range, and lifted his own blade, ready to strike back. But then something odd caught his eye. *What's that?* A strange, dark shape hovered above the palace turrets. Before he could look closer, Tom felt his legs swept out from under him.

"Oof!" The cobbles punched the air from his lungs. He blinked up to see Amelia grinning down at him, the tip of her sword planted squarely in his chest. Whatever the dark shape had been, it had vanished.

"Had enough yet?" Amelia asked.

Tom nodded. "I yield." A cheer went up from the crowd as Amelia stuck out her hand and helped Tom to his feet.

She leaned in close as he stood. "You didn't have to let me win, you know," she murmured.

"I didn't," Tom said. "I took my eye off the duel. You were the better fighter today." A fierce blush crept over Amelia's cheeks.

A hush fell over the crowd as Queen Irina, dressed in a flowing blue sorceress's gown with long, bell-shaped sleeves, rose from her throne. Tom and Amelia dropped to their knees as the witch-queen crossed the courtyard with Freya at her side. Freya's dark hair fell loose around her shoulders, and a proud smile lit her face. The two women stopped before Tom and Amelia, and Irina gestured for them to stand.

"Well fought!" the queen said. "It is good to know we have two such talented warriors to protect Gwildor and Avantia."

"Yes – congratulations for putting on such a wonderful display!" Freya said.

"It is you who should be congratulated, Mother," Tom said, "for teaching Amelia so well."

Freya gazed wistfully at Tom for a moment. "Oh, Tom!" she said. "How long will you stay with us this time?"

Tom glanced down at the ground.

"I'll be leaving for Avantia tomorrow," he said. "But I'll miss you."

BOOM! Tom lurched sideways and almost toppled as the ground leapt beneath his feet. Adrenaline rushed through his veins as screams of terror rang out all around him. He turned to see a cloud of dust hanging above a crater blown in the cobbles.

"We're under attack!" Amelia cried, just as a huge shadow fell upon them from above, draining the colour from the square. Tom looked up to see the curved wooden hull of a ship – a *flying* ship – blocking out the sky. Squat black cannons poked from holes that ran along the keel, and a grinning Beast-skull figurehead jutted from the prow. Along the length of the gunwale,

fierce tattooed faces scowled down at them as ropes unfurled towards the ground.

"Prepare to be flattened, you puny weevils," rang out a harsh cry over the courtyard.

The Pirates of Makai!

PIRATE ATTACK

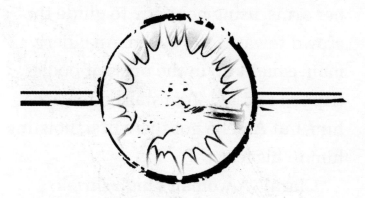

BOOM! The flying ship's cannons
all fired at once, sending up puffs
of smoke. Tom leapt towards Queen
Irina and threw up his shield.
CRASH! Chips of rock clattered
against the wood. Dust and debris
filled the air and courtiers ran
screaming in every direction.

"Evacuate the square! This way!"
the queen cried, diving from the

cover of Tom's shield and pointing towards an archway. Freya spread her arms, using her body to guide the crowd towards the queen. An elderly man, caught up in the press of bodies, tripped and fell. Tom started towards him, but Amelia got there first, hoisting him to his feet.

"Clara!" A woman's high shriek pierced through the clamour. Tom turned to see a dark-haired woman with a plump baby in her arms staring across the square, her eyes wide with horror. He followed her gaze to see a small girl, no more than three, crouched in the shadow of the courtyard wall.

She'll be killed! Tom ducked his head and barrelled across the courtyard. He

scooped the child up just as another
terrific crash rang out from above.
Chunks of stone battered his tunic as
he leapt away from the wall, shielding
the child with his body. When the dust
cleared, Tom found the girl's mother
hurrying towards him. "Quickly," he

cried, jerking his head towards the exit. She turned, her toddler staring round-eyed over her shoulder. Tom kept close behind the woman, holding her child tightly, until they reached Queen Irina. When Tom set the girl down, she buried her face in her mother's skirt.

The woman clutched Tom's arm. "Thank you!" she said, before Irina ushered her after the last few courtiers through the archway.

More black missiles plummeted down. Bricks exploded in every direction from the courtyard walls. Above the racket of falling stone, Tom heard a terrified whinny. A horse tethered at the base of a tower bucked and reared, its eyes rolling. A huge

hole gaped in the tower wall behind
it, and Tom could see cracks running
upwards through the brickwork. *The
tower's going to fall!* Freya leapt to
the horse's side and sliced through
the animal's tether with her sword.
The horse lurched away just as a
huge section of tower wall broke free.

"Look out!" Tom cried. It was too
late. His heart squeezed with horror
as a brick glanced off Freya's temple
and she crumpled to the ground.

Tom raced to his mother and threw
up his shield to protect them both.
He pulled her free of the rubble,
carrying her to the shelter of the
archway where Queen Irina waited,
then set her down. As Irina bent
to check Freya's breathing, Tom

watched, sick with fear.

"Tom, look out!" Amelia cried. Tom spun as something huge and black flashed towards him. *Boof!* Heavy boots thudded into his chest, throwing him backwards. Tom landed in a roll and jumped up just in time to see a pirate leap down on to the cobbles from a rope. More tattooed pirates were swarming down lanyards from the ship, dropping into the square. Irina stood before his mother's body, her magical staff raised.

Amelia lunged for the nearest invader – a huge brute with so many tattoos, his skin looked blue. With a lazy smile, the pirate swung his cutlass, slicing her wooden sword in half. Amelia let out a scream of rage, ducked her head and charged, ramming the big man hard in the gut. He doubled over, puffing and blowing, while Amelia snatched the cutlass from his hand.

Tom advanced on the pirate who'd kicked him – a leathery-skinned man with blackened stumps for teeth.

"After another thrashing, are you?" the pirate asked with a leer. Then he stabbed his cutlass at Tom's chest. Tom blocked with his shield and swung his wooden sword high, cracking the pirate across the side of the head. The man dropped like a stone. Tom bent and prised the cutlass from his hand. *Not as good as my own sword, but it'll have to do.*

He scanned the chaos in the square,

looking for his next target. Amelia
hacked and jabbed at two skinny,
tattooed youths at once, driving them
backwards over the rubble. Irina still
shielded Freya, wielding her staff.
CRACK! She sent a sizzling ball of
energy towards a broad-chested man
with an axe, throwing him backwards

into two more pirates and knocking them down like skittles.

Tom felt a flicker of relief as he saw the queen's guard pouring through the courtyard gate. Longswords clanged against cutlasses as the armoured guards met the pirate attack. But everywhere Tom looked, still more pirates slid down ropes into the square.

"To the dungeons!" bellowed a giant man with a scarred hole instead of a nose. *They're here to free Sanpao!* Tom realised with a stab of alarm. He looked over at the palace and spotted a slender, hooded figure slipping through the gateway. *No, you don't!*

Tom lifted his shield and barged across the courtyard, dodging beneath flashing blades and ducking through the archway into the palace gardens. Ahead, the intruder was already heading through the palace doors. Tom followed close behind into the dimly lit quiet of the entrance hall. He tiptoed after the cloaked stranger, along a corridor, then down a spiral staircase to a branching stone passageway that ran beneath the palace. The hooded figure moved quickly through the shadows, but instead of taking the turning for the dungeons, they hurried straight on, towards the heavy metal door to the treasury. Tom pressed himself against the wall and watched as the slender figure stooped and blew some sort of powder into the lock. With a flash of purple light, the door swung open. The intruder stepped inside.

Tom burst through the doorway, cutlass raised, to find the stranger bent over a crystal display case filled with glittering jewels.

"Step away from the queen's treasure," Tom growled.

"I only want one," the intruder answered in a high, female voice. She turned, her face cast into shadow by her deep hood, then slipped a hand into her cloak…

Tom lunged, but before he could reach the girl, a long cat-o'-nine-tails, crackling with glowing blue energy, lashed towards him. Tom felt a blaze of pain in his arm as the whip struck. His legs folded, suddenly rubbery and

numb. He tried to rise, but none of his
muscles would obey.

I'm paralysed!

Tom watched, seething with
helpless fury as the thief plucked a
large, pale jewel from the display
case. *The Pearl of Gwildor!* Tom

realised, as the girl slipped the magical artefact into the folds of her cloak.

"See you later," she sang out tauntingly, then she hurried away through the open door.

CELL BREAK

Deep in the dungeons below the palace, Sanpao pushed his body up off the filthy cobbles again and again. *Ninety-seven… Ninety-eight…* His knuckles smarted and his arm muscles burned with the effort, but it felt good. *Ninety-nine*, he counted. A bead of sweat fell in his eye, making it sting. *One hundred!* Sanpao heaved himself over and sat with his knees bent up to his chest for a moment, breathing heavily, staring at the cell's slimy wall. Tally marks covered the damp stone. He'd given up making them long ago. But he hadn't given up on his fitness regime. He ate the slops they gave him, he slept, and he kept himself strong. So, when he finally escaped, he would be able to keelhaul the lot of them.

A sudden sound made Sanpao catch his breath – a muffled boom followed by distant screams. He tipped his head, listening intently. More screams – falling rubble – the clash of steel. For the first time in what felt like a long, long while, Sanpao smiled. *Ha ha! So, Queen Irina the Snooty is finally under attack, is she? I wonder whose nose she's got up this time? And, more to the point, I wonder how much it will cost me to buy my way into their good books.* Sanpao rubbed his calloused hands together. *I could make a new king very rich with all the treasure I've—*

CRASH! The door of his cell slammed open and two of the biggest, ugliest brutes Sanpao had ever set eyes on burst into the room. Both wore filthy leathers and scuffed knee-high boots. One had a twisted scar instead of a right eye, and the other had a tattoo of a serpent running up his face. Sanpao got to his feet, grinning.

"If it isn't One-Eye and The Knobbler!" he said. "What took you so long, eh?"

"We're here now, aren't we?" said The

Knobbler. He jerked a thumb towards the door. "Come on, boss. Let's get out of here before the guards work out what we're up to!" Sanpao didn't need telling twice. He hurried after his two oldest crew members, along a passage, up a winding stair, and finally out into the sun. The square before him was teeming with his own men. More pirates stood on the battlements of the wall. Sanpao's ship hung in the air above them, while Irina's soldiers cowered in a huddle behind a pile of rubble that looked like it had recently been a tower. Sanpao let out a hearty chuckle. *Ha ha! That's what you get for locking me up!*

"Got him," One-Eye shouted up

at the ship. It sailed lower, almost touching down in the square. Sanpao leapt on to the ship's wooden steps and climbed up on to the deck. A slim figure in a long cloak stood above him on the quarterdeck at the wheel.

"Kensa!" Sanpao cried. *I knew she wouldn't just leave me to rot!* The figure turned and threw back its hood, revealing a smooth, young face, studded with metal piercings and overshadowed by a bright red Mohawk. Sanpao gaped in surprise to see not his wife, but his daughter.

"Ria!" he said, at last. "Come to rescue your old papa, have you? Did your mother send you?"

The girl shrugged. "She wasn't really interested in breaking you out, I'm afraid. She doesn't even know I'm here."

"Well, you came, and that's what counts," Sanpao said, flashing his daughter what he hoped looked like a warm smile. "And I promise I'll steal you something pretty to thank you now I'm back where I belong at the helm." But as he started up the quarterdeck steps, his daughter's green eyes narrowed and she stepped forwards, blocking the way.

"Why don't you get something to eat and take a rest?" she said. "I've got everything under control here." Then she wrinkled her nose at Sanpao. "And maybe have a wash while you're at it – you stink worse than a dead squid on a hot day."

Sanpao paused. His palms itched
to be back on the wheel of his ship.
But it had been a long time since he'd
had a decent meal. He looked at his
skinny slip of a daughter, dressed

from head to toe in black leathers, pretending to be all grown up, and grinned.

"Fine," he said. "You keep the wheel for now – but only until I've recovered from being stuck in that stinking cell."

Sanpao turned. In a blur of motion, a booted foot slammed into his face. He staggered back, eyes watering, to see a scowling girl with long blonde hair drop from a rope on to the deck before him. The girl lifted a cutlass and charged. Sanpao leapt aside. "Where'd she come from?" he cried, ducking behind a barrel as the girl swiped again.

"Tom's pesky friend," Ria growled. She raised her voice to shriek at the crew. "How did none of you useless rot-for-brains notice she'd sneaked on board? Deal with her – now!" Sanpao found himself grinning, even as he dodged another of the angry girl's strikes. *Ria's taking after her papa nicely!*

A pair of spotty lads who looked barely old enough to wipe their own noses leapt out behind the blonde girl. She spun round and clapped the lankier of the two over the side of the skull with the butt of her sword. The kid staggered back, clutching his head. The other swung his cutlass. The dark girl met the blow, knocked it aside, then jabbed for his ribs. The boy just managed to dodge, but the girl kicked him in the shins, making him hop backwards, howling.

She ain't a bad fighter, this one,
thought Sanpao in surprise.

As the girl closed on the lanky boy
she'd kicked, cutlass raised, Sanpao
spotted One-Eye and The Knobbler
coming at her, one from either side.
One-Eye grabbed hold of her wrist,

twisting it so she gasped and dropped her blade. The Knobbler stepped in, tossing her over his shoulder as if she weighed less than a cat. He carried her to where One-Eye waited with a length of rope.

Sanpao turned away, leaving One-Eye and The Knobbler to their work. "Right, lads!" he called to his crew. "To the cannons. We're going to bomb the city to dust!"

Not one of the crew shifted. Instead, they all turned their gaze up towards the quarterdeck, where Ria stood leaning against the wheel, grinning.

"Leave the city to rot," Ria said. "We've got bigger fish to fry. Man the sails! We're heading east!"

4

THE AVANTIAN FLEET

Here we go again, Elenna thought, letting out a sigh as Admiral Ryker stopped for about the hundredth time that morning. He frowned through his monocle at a young, red-haired sailor. The sailor stood to attention by the mainsail of the ship, his eyes screwed up against the sun and his hand raised in a neat salute.

"Midshipman Anders, straighten that sash!" Ryker barked. "And stop squinting, will you? You look like a fool!"

"Yes, Admiral," the young man shouted, clicking his heels together.

"And those boots need polishing," Ryker bellowed. "You are a disgrace!"

Elenna couldn't see anything wrong

with the sailor's boots, but she bit her tongue.

"Yes, Admiral!" the sailor replied.

Elenna glanced down at the vast ledger in her hands, and sighed again. They'd been all over every ship in the fleet, ticking off the barrels of salt pork and tack in the holds, along with kegs of beer, bolts of sailcloth, coiled ropes and stacks of cannonballs. They'd inspected the mess hall and cabins, the galleys and the gundecks. Ryker had found fault with just about everything and everyone, from lieutenants to carpenters to the lowliest ship's boys. Now just the final inspection remained – and Elenna couldn't wait for it to be over. With King Hugo and Queen Aroha busy with their new baby, Prince Thomas, it had fallen to her to oversee the final touches to Avantia's new fleet. *I'd rather be fighting Beasts.*

"Call that a knot?" Ryker bellowed, snapping her out of her train of thought. He was pointing straight at her uncle, who was busy fixing the last sail to the mizzenmast.

"It's a good one, sir!" Leo answered, giving the knot a sharp tug. Elenna's uncle was the most skilled boatman she knew, and he had volunteered to help with the fleet free of charge.

"Not good enough!" Ryker snapped. "Tie it again."

Elenna managed to catch her uncle's eye. "Sorry!" she mouthed. But Leo just smiled, his eyes twinkling, and calmly started untying the knot. *You've got to pick your battles, Elenna*, she could almost hear him saying inside her head. She took a deep breath, forcing her hunched shoulders to relax. But, though her anger faded, she couldn't shift the nagging worry that she'd been carrying inside her for days. Another of her uncle's sayings flashed through her mind – *always listen to your gut*. And Elenna's gut was telling her something bad was going to happen.

As if right on cue, a clamour of cries and the shuffle of boots started up on the poop deck, making Elenna's heart skip. She looked up to see the crew backing away from a swirling column of blue smoke as tall as a man.

"Fire!" someone cried. But the smoke quickly cleared as if a breeze had shifted it all at once, leaving a flickering image of Tom. *A message from Gwildor!* Elenna strode across the deck and took the steps up to the poop deck two at a time. As she drew closer to the image, the knot of worry in her guts tightened. *Tom looks grey!* In a four-poster bed behind him, Elenna could see what looked like the sleeping form of his mother.

"Tom, what's happened?" Elenna asked. "Is Freya all right?"

"We were attacked by the Pirates of Makai," Tom said, wearily. "Mother was knocked out during the battle." Elenna heard a catch in his voice. "She hasn't yet woken up. It's been a while now,

and I am worried…" With a pang,
Elenna wished she could be with Tom
to offer him support.

"Irina will give her the best care,"
Elenna said.

Tom took a deep breath and
nodded, but his face didn't brighten.
"There's something else," he said.

"During the attack, someone freed Sanpao from his cell."

"Kensa?" Elenna asked.

"I don't know," Tom said. "There was woman in a cloak – she stole the Pearl of Gwildor. It could have been Kensa, but I'm not sure. Anyway, it gets worse. Amelia's missing…"

"I'll send my fleet at once!" Ryker boomed from right behind Elenna, making her jump.

Tom shook his head. "I'm grateful for the offer, Admiral, but for now, it is better if Elenna goes on ahead to Gwildor. At least until we know what we're dealing with. It will be safer and quicker that way."

"How could Elenna possibly be quicker than my fleet?" Ryker

bellowed. "My ships are the fastest in all the kingdoms. Nothing comes close!"

A flicker of something approaching a grin crossed Tom's worried face. "I wouldn't be so sure!" He touched a shiny green scale in his shield.

The boat gave a lurch. Water droplets scattered down all around them, sparkling in the sun. "What?!" Ryker cried, grabbing Elenna's arm, as Sepron the Sea Serpent's magnificent emerald-green head appeared above the gunwale. Elenna prised herself free of Ryker's panicked grip and pressed her ledger into his hands.

"You'll need to complete the inspection without me, Admiral,"

Elenna said. The man's mouth opened and shut like a goldfish as he stared at the Beast, but he didn't say anything.

"Looks like you're going to have quite a ride," Elenna's uncle said, nodding towards the serpent. He smiled, opening his arms wide, and Elenna stepped into them, letting her uncle fold her in a tight hug. "Good luck," Leo said, releasing her. "Now go and give those pirates what for!"

Elenna climbed up on to the gunwale and dropped down on to Sepron's broad green back. She clung tight to the Beast's neck ruff and braced herself.

"I… Is that thing safe?" asked Ryker. Elenna's stomach somersaulted as

the Beast shot forwards. Wind, wet with salty spray, buffeted against her. She leant into it, grinning as they raced over the ocean.

I might be headed into danger – but at least I'm leaving Ryker behind!

5

RACE TO THE COAST

Busy fishing villages passed by in a blur as Tom rode across Gwildor. Flame, Freya's stallion, was the quickest in the kingdom, but Tom used the magical speed of Tagus's horseshoe to drive him faster still.

All the time, he watched the flying ship, an ugly dark blot, as it flew towards the shimmering sea.

I've got to reach it before it's above the water.

A narrow line of flowering trees fringed the beach, and a long stone jetty reached from the golden sands into the calm Gwildorian ocean.

Tom gripped Flame's flanks with his knees, and took one hand off the reins, touching his fingers to the red jewel in his belt. *Krabb!* Tom called to the Good Beast with his mind. *I need you.*

Wind whipped past him as they thundered down to the beach and over the sparkling sands. The ship ahead was over the water already, so Tom pulled Flame to a halt beside the stone jetty and leapt down. "Home!" he told the horse, knowing it would find its way back to its mistress. Then Tom sprang into a run, sprinting along the jetty as fast as he could. Waves crashed against the stone, sending up a dazzling rainbow mist. The wind buffeted him from every direction.

As Tom reached the end of the jetty, he called on the power of his golden boots and launched himself into the air, making a grab for the tip of the rudder. *Yes!* His arm muscles took up the strain as he jerked to a stop. He heaved himself upwards until his feet met the wood. Then he edged sideways and started to climb.

As Tom neared the gunwale, he could hear cheers and singing coming from below decks, along with the thud of tankards on wood. He pulled himself up to peer over the rail. His

heart leapt as he spotted Amelia
seated at the base of the mainmast,
her arms tied to the thick pole
behind her. *So that's where she got
to! Kidnapped!* She squirmed and
twisted, her face contorting with

fury as she tried to get free. A couple of pirates lolled drunkenly against barrels behind her, and a bleary-eyed man holding a tankard stood at the wheel. Otherwise, the main deck was deserted. *They must be celebrating...*

Tom thought. *Which suits me fine.*

Tom vaulted silently up on to the gunwale, then leapt up to grab the rigging for the mizzenmast. Swinging from rope to rope, he crossed the decks, passing over the drunken pirates' heads. Two more leaps, and Tom dropped lightly on to the main deck before Amelia. She fell still at once, her eyes widening with surprise. Tom put a finger to his lips, then skirted behind her to untie the rope.

Before he could work the stiff knot loose, Amelia let out a gasp. Tom looked up to see two huge pirates spring towards him from either side – one a bald-headed brute with a messy scar in place of an eye, the other with a snake tattoo over half his face. Tom shot to his feet, reaching for his sword, but before he could draw it, tough hands gripped his arms and tossed him over Amelia's head. He landed in a heap at the feet of a slender, cloaked figure holding a cat-o'-nine-tails. *The thief from the palace*, Tom realised with dread, as he remembered the crippling touch of her whip.

As Tom rose, the figure lowered her hood, and Tom found himself face to face with a wiry girl about his own age. Bright red hair stood up like a parrot's crest down the middle of her shaven head, and silver piercings glittered in her eyebrows and ears.

The girl smiled, then shook her head, tutting softly. "If it isn't Avantia's favourite hero," she said, her green eyes glinting. "Mama and Sanpao used to tell me all about your annoying antics. Somehow, I had expected someone a bit…brawnier. My name is Ria, by the way." She lifted her whip almost lazily and cracked it against the deck, leaving a sooty scar. "I'm going to do something my parents never could. I'm going to rid Avantia of her so-called champion once and for all. I challenge you to a duel!"

Anger filled Tom. "A duel? As if any daughter of Sanpao and Kensa would ever know how to fight fair!"

Ria shrugged. "The choice is yours. Fight me, or walk the plank."

"Fine!" Tom said, sinking into a fighting stance and lifting his sword. Ria's grin broadened. She brandished

her whip, and Tom swallowed hard as
he saw how each of the nine leather
tails sizzled with energy.

"Tom! Look out!" Amelia cried.
Tom turned to see a huge dark shape

blocking his view. He registered a scowling tattooed face, a club…then, *BANG!* Pain and light exploded inside his skull. The deck slammed into his cheek before he even knew he was falling. He tried to lift his head but could barely open his eyes. *Sanpao hit me!*

"What did you do that for?" Tom heard Ria screech through the thudding pain in his head. "I wanted to beat him fairly!"

"You should be thanking me," Sanpao growled. "He'd have won. Tom always wins. He's lucky that way!"

Tom forced his eyes to open but everything whirled by in a blur. His body seemed to be pressed against the deck by the spinning inside his head.

"Well, I guess it's done now," Ria snapped, "but I'm not happy. Lads – get rid of that mess, will you?"

Tom heard the scrape of boots on the deck. Meaty hands gripped his arms and legs, lifting him up. He felt a whoosh of wind and his stomach swooped. *I'm falling...* The waves rushed towards him and he couldn't even get into a diving position.

SPLASH! Cold water closed around him, driving the air from his lungs. He tried to pump his arms and legs, but his heavy limbs wouldn't obey. He opened his eyes a crack to see the bright surface receding, the shafts of sunlight getting fainter as he sank down into the darkness.

I'm going to drown...

6

DIVING FOR TREASURE

"Stop sulking, Ria," Sanpao snapped at his daughter. "That boy's been a dead man walking since he got me slammed in that cell. And now he's gone, we can do what we like."

Ria's scowl only deepened as she looked at the spot where Tom had entered the sea. "There is such a thing as honour, you know, even among pirates. But I guess you wouldn't understand that, would you, Sanpao?"

Sanpao's temper flared. "Show some respect, you ungrateful brat! I'm your father, after all."

Ria rolled her eyes and let out a theatrical sigh. Then she turned her back on him and strode towards the stern.

Sanpao followed his daughter up on to the poop deck. He found her gazing out to sea, a map unfurled between her hands. Peering over her shoulder, Sanpao noticed the craggy coastline wasn't one he recognised. *What's she up to?*

One of Ria's spotty new lads appeared from below decks and approached them, holding out a polished brass astrolabe.

Sanpao grabbed the shiny disc and held it up to the horizon. "Right, now we can set a course for—"

Ria snatched the instrument and gave it back to the boy at her side. "We'll set a course for here," she said,

planting her finger in the centre of her map, where a large red *X* had been scrawled between a pair of small islands. "That's where the greatest treasure of them all will be found." Ria turned to face the crew. "Weigh anchor and hoist the mizzen!"

As the crew sprang into action, Sanpao growled at his daughter: "It can't be the greatest treasure of all, or I'd have heard of it, wouldn't I?" He took a breath, and tried to sweeten his voice. "Look, now you've broken your old dad out of prison, we should do some real plundering, eh? Not go hunting after some cheap trinket."

Ria didn't even look at Sanpao. "Bring her down low to the waves!" she called to the crew.

Sanpao felt his stomach drop as the ship started to lose height fast. *What's she doing bossing my crew about?* Soon they were skimming along just above the waves. To either side of them a small, jagged-edged island jutted up from the waves – just like the ones on the map. Ria gave a signal, and the ship drew to a halt.

Sanpao gazed down at the gentle, sapphire-blue waves. "It'd be a brave pirate to dive here," he said. "Gwildor's ocean might look like a millpond compared to the seas back home, but mark my words – it's infested with sharks. And worse!"

"Well, it's a good job you're such a fast swimmer then," Ria said, smiling sweetly at him.

"Hey? Me?" said Sanpao.

Ria held out her hand and nodded pointedly towards the huge pearl cradled in her palm. *The Pearl of Gwildor!* Sanpao knew the magical jewel would allow a swimmer to breathe underwater.

He took a step back, shaking his head. "No way… I'm not diving in there!"

Ria's smile didn't falter. "Oh? But there's a jewel-encrusted sword on the seabed, worth more than all the treasure you've ever found. Plus, it will make the Pirates of Makai more powerful than ever!"

"That's all very well," Sanpao told her. "But I'm the Pirate King. A king doesn't go swimming to the bottom of

the sea at his daughter's say-so."

Sanpao's skin prickled as he noticed an unnatural silence all around him. He looked up to see his crew – every maggot-eating one of them – glaring back at him. *Darn it all if she hasn't*

nicked my men! he realised, not sure
whether to feel angry or proud.

"I'll give you a choice," Ria said.
"You can dive for the treasure with
the Pearl of Gwildor –" she glanced
at the jewel once more – "or The
Knobbler and One-Eye can chuck
you over the side without it."

With the eyes of the crew all on
him, Sanpao saw he had no choice.
He snatched the pearl. "You could
have just asked me nicely," he snarled.

Ria smiled. "Oh, but Papa, I didn't
need to ask, because we both know
you're the only pirate brave enough to
pull this off!"

Sanpao tried to look stern, but he
couldn't quite hold back a smile.
She's as crafty as her mother!

Gripping the pearl tightly in his hand, Sanpao heaved himself up on to the gunwale, angled his arms down towards the water, and dived.

Sploosh! Bubbles swirled around him and his ears popped as he swam down through the clear water. When his breath ran out, he felt a stab of panic, but he forced himself to take another breath, knowing that the pearl would keep him safe.

He kicked hard, forcing himself deeper, marvelling at the fact that he could breathe as easily as if he were on land – not only that, but the pearl gave off a silvery glow, lighting the way. When he reached the seabed, he glanced about. *So, where's this fancy sword then?* Fine sand glittered in

the light from the pearl, and dark
ridges of rock, crawling with crabs
and brittle stars, poked up from the
seabed. *Ah ha!* The familiar glint of
treasure caught his eye.

Sanpao swam in for a closer look.

A long sword with the biggest, shiniest purple gemstone he had ever seen embedded in the hilt, stuck up from the seabed. The blade had been driven halfway into a ridge of stone. *What a beauty!* Sanpao gripped the hilt

with his free hand and gave it a tug. Nothing happened. He pulled again.

Cursed thing won't budge! As a last resort, he pressed both his feet against rock, clenched his teeth and yanked. The sword slid free, and Sanpao tumbled backwards, spinning over in the water. He righted himself and ran his eyes down the treasure in his hands. The metal gleamed as if newly forged. *This gemstone must be worth at least...*

Suddenly, a swirling current stirred the ocean around him. Sanpao glanced down to see silt rising from the seabed, clouding the water. A tingle of fear ran down his spine as the dark ridges of rock started to move, flexing against each other.

Pebbles and sand slid away revealing more dark purplish rock. *Not rock...* Sanpao realised with a jolt of terror. *It's the shell of a Beast!*

Sanpao kicked his legs harder than ever before towards the surface.

THE STORM KING

Tom sank deeper and deeper, the
icy water all around him numbing
his muscles so he could hardly feel
his own body. As the last glimmer
of light from the surface faded to a
soft amber glow, he let his eyes fall
shut. His lungs ached for breath but,
in the darkness and watery quiet, he
felt sleepy, and strangely calm. Hazy
thoughts swam in his mind. *I hope*

someone finds my sword and shield after I'm gone…

Then suddenly, the water stirred. A gravelly voice spoke into Tom's mind, jolting him awake. *I'm coming!* Tom blinked, trying to focus in the dimness. Through his muddled senses, he thought he could see a dark shape, speeding towards him. A cloud of bubbles surged over him, and a strong current tugged at his limbs. *Whoosh!* Something huge and solid lifted him up, carrying him faster and faster towards the surface.

A moment later, Tom burst out into sunlight. He took a huge shuddering breath, then another. He lifted his spinning head, pushing himself up on his elbows, and found he was lying on

Krabb's broad, knobbly back. *Thank you, friend*, he told the Good Beast, letting his head sink back on to the creature's shell. *You saved my life!* Gratitude washed through him as the feeling flowed back into his limbs.

But then a powerful surge of dread and worry jolted him upright. *I have to save Amelia!*

Tom scanned the ocean. *There!* The pirate ship hovered in the distance between a pair of tiny islands. It hung so close to the water that waves slapped against its hull. Putting his hand to the red jewel in his belt, Tom asked Krabb to carry him closer. He crouched low as the Good Beast moved smoothly and silently through the ocean. Nearing the hovering vessel, Tom saw a bearded, tattooed swimmer surface alongside the keel, waving an arm frantically. *Sanpao!* Tom ducked down out of sight as far as he could, watching as the pirate lifted the other hand from the water, revealing a long, glinting sword.

"Got it!" Sanpao bellowed up to the ship. "Now get me out of here!" A group of youthful faces appeared at the gunwale. Tom recognised Ria and some of her crew. A tall pirate, clad all in black, shimmied down a rope and snatched the sword from Sanpao. Two more pirates quickly hauled the youth back into the ship.

"Oi!" Sanpao hollered. "What about me? There's a Beast down here—"

The ocean ahead suddenly erupted like a volcano then crashed down over Tom. He blinked away salt water to see a colossal lobster with a gnarled, dark shell the purplish grey of a storm cloud filling his view. Long antennae quivered above glowing

yellow eyes that glared straight at him. Each of the monster's huge front legs ended in a pair of gaping, segmented pincers. Glancing up at the pirate ship, Tom saw Ria's lips spread in a wide, cruel grin. The girl lifted her hand and Tom saw she was clutching the silver sword.

As she did so, the Beast's antennae started to shudder. A hideous droning sound filled the air, like the sickening buzz of a million wasps. Tom had to fight to stop himself crumpling into a ball. He clamped his hands to his ears only to hear the same dizzying hum inside his head. *I am Verak, the Storm King! I have awoken to serve my new master. Any who harm the bearer of the Jewelled Sword shall die!*

As the hideous buzzing fell silent, a sudden gust of wind almost snatched Tom from Krabb's back. In an instant, the bright sea darkened to grey. The air crackled with energy, and as Tom glanced up, he felt a thrill of dread. Huge anvil-shaped thunderclouds towered in the sky, swelling by the moment. The pirate ship rose, sails billowing, to hang above Verak's head.

The Beast's bright eyes swivelled upwards. Four massive claws snapped up at the pirate ship's hull.

"Give it a rest, will you!" Ria shouted over the gunwale. She lifted her arm and pointed her gleaming sword down at the Beast. *The Jewelled Sword!* Tom realised, noticing the huge purple gemstone in the hilt. Verak's clutching pincer fell still and he settled back into the water, his glowing eyes fixed on the girl with the sword.

She's controlling the Beast!

Krabb's low, rasping voice spoke into Tom's mind. *This is a dark day for Gwildor*, he said. *I have battled the storm king before. The whole of Gwildor was very nearly destroyed.*

In the murky light of the gathering storm, Tom ran his eyes over Verak, taking in the dark bulk of his great shell and snapping claws. With a shudder, he remembered the terrible blast of noise the Beast had made, almost bringing him to his knees. He felt suddenly small and weak, but drew his shoulders back and took a deep breath. *We don't have to defeat the Beast – we just have to get the sword.* He touched the red jewel again. *Krabb – attack the pirate ship!*

As Krabb surged through the water, the pirates saw him coming and began to point and holler.

"Chop him to pieces!" Tom heard Ria shriek. The Beast came alive at once, feelers twitching angrily. Tom crouched low on Krabb's rough back, feet spread wide for balance. As soon as the lobster's purple bulk came within reach, Tom leapt up and swung his blade. *CRACK!* The shock of the blow jolted up his arm but didn't leave a mark on the Beast. *That shell's like stone!*

Verak's vast double-clawed pincer

lashed out. In a blur of speed, Krabb's club-like forelimb snapped towards it. With a crash that threw Tom to his knees, the two Beasts' pincers locked together in a mighty battle of strength. Verak's yellow eyes burned with fury. His whipping antennae started to vibrate, the wall of sound almost knocking Tom off his feet. He dropped on to all fours to keep from falling into the sea. As the hideous sound went on, Krabb's vast body began to shudder, his claw still locked with Verak's pincer. Tom could feel the Good Beast's strength ebbing away.

Verak tugged his claw free of Krabb's weakened grip and snapped at the Good Beast's limb. *SNICK!* Krabb let out a keening cry of rage

and pain as his yellow claw plunged
into the sea.

Verak's eyes flashed with triumph
as he started at Tom. Tom lifted his
shield and tightened his grip on his
sword, but he knew neither could

withstand many blows from the Beast's double claws.

He gritted his teeth and braced his muscles anyway. *This may be my last battle, but while there's blood in my veins, I will fight!*

STORY TWO

WAR ON THE WAVES

Verak is even more terrifying than I hoped. And with the Jewelled Sword in my grasp, he obeys my every command. Oh, the fun I will have!

My father never liked to talk about Tom of Avantia, and now I see why. He does have a knack of showing up when he's least wanted. What are the chances that he was in Gwildor's capital the very day I launched my attack?

No matter, though – it has turned out rather well. Tom has come to me, and it looks like I will finish the business Sanpao never could. And what better place to watch Tom perish than from the deck of my ship? Verak's claws will tear him into pieces so small the fish won't even have to chew.

And after that, Avantia will be without a protector. The kingdom will be as open as a dead clam, its pearls ripe for picking!

Your Captain, Ria

1

BATTLE OF THE BEASTS

Sepron carried Elenna over the waves so fast she could hardly catch her breath. Her hands and arms ached with the strain of clinging tight to the Beast's scaled back, and salty spray drenched her to the skin. Clear blue sky arched overhead, but on the horizon, vast grey thunderheads churned, climbing higher, casting deep shadows over the ocean below. *There's nothing natural about that storm!* Elenna thought. *I hope we're not too late.*

Soon, gusts of wind tore angrily at Elenna's hair and clothes and choppy waves buffeted Sepron's hide, soaking Elenna over and over. As they drew closer to the gathering storm, Elenna spotted a shape hanging in the darkening sky between a pair of forested islands not far from the Gwildorian coast. *Sanpao's pirate ship!* Suddenly a terrible noise hit her, a grating, sickening buzz that felt like it was right inside her head. Wincing with pain, she scanned the shadowy water below the ship and made out the dark forms of two enormous sea Beasts.

Elenna recognised Krabb's broad yellowish back, but something was wrong – the Good Beast seemed hunched up, his jointed legs and feelers tucked defensively towards his body as he reeled away from a huge lobster with a purplish-black shell and bright yellow eyes. Elenna gasped with horror as she closed in on the Beasts. Tom lay prone on Krabb's back. *He's hurt!*

Sepron let out an angry roar and darted forwards. Elenna clung on for her life as Sepron's massive tail lashed through the ocean, creating a towering tidal wave. As the wall of water slammed into the giant lobster, the horrible buzzing sound stopped. The wave lifted the purple Beast up, forcing it away from Krabb. Sepron knifed between the two Beasts, drawing up alongside Tom.

Elenna let out a breath of relief as Tom scrambled up into a crouch. "Nice timing!" he called. "I thought I was finished!" He pointed up at Sanpao's ship, hanging ominously above them. "The pirates are commanding that lobster Beast... It's called Verak."

"Well, we've got two Beasts – they've only got one!" Elenna said. But as the colossal lobster veered back towards them, snapping four club-like claws each as big as an ox, her heart clenched with fear. Sepron let out a roar and shot through the waves towards the Beast, which lifted a giant purple forelimb. *BOOF!*

Sepron barged head-first into the pincer, batting it aside.

Krabb charged past with a hiss of rage. Crouched on the Good Beast's back, Tom swung his sword. The blade rebounded from the lobster's shell and Tom staggered back.

Elenna's stomach lurched and she

almost lost her grip, her whole body tingling with the shock of speed as Sepron reared then surged towards Verak. The serpent snapped at the purple lobster's front limb, but the Evil Beast snatched it away, his antennae quivering with rage. Then with a flick of his broad, fanned tail, the Beast dived, vanishing beneath the waves. A trail of bubbles left in Verak's wake led towards the Gwildorian shoreline.

Tom drew up alongside Elenna on Krabb. "The Beast won't give up for long," he said, "Sanpao's been freed – but Ria, his crazy daughter, is in charge now. And she's got a magical sword that controls Verak."

Elenna watched the huge pirate ship

sailing through the air after Verak towards the Gwildorian shore. With a thrill of fear, she spotted a girl with a red mohawk glaring back at them.

BOOM! A cannon poking from the pirate ship's keel recoiled with a puff of smoke. Water erupted in a towering cascade before them.

They're shooting at us!

"Tom – Krabb's injured," Elenna said, shuffling back on Sepron's scales to make room. "Come with me."

Tom nodded and laid a hand on the Good Beast's shell. "Thank you, old friend. Get yourself to safety."

He leapt from Krabb's back on to Sepron. Krabb's legs flicked and he sank out of sight just as another huge bang rang out from above. Elenna clung to Sepron's scales as they shot away, skimming over the stormy sea. Cannonballs plunged into the waves behind them, but Sepron sped onwards, only stopping when they were well out of range.

"How can we fight from out here?" Elenna cried.

Tom suddenly sat upright and pointed. "Are those Avantian ships I can see?"

Elenna followed the line of his finger, and groaned. In the brighter water beyond the forested islands, a dozen ships, their sails billowing in the strengthening wind, cut towards them. "Yes," Elenna said, sighing. "I had hoped Admiral Ryker would stay back in Avantia." As she gazed at the Avantian armada speeding their way, she saw a puff of smoke as a cannon fired. A black missile whizzed overhead towards the pirate ship near the shoreline, plunging down into the shallows just short of its mark.

"No!" Tom gasped. "Amelia's on board that ship! We have to tell them to stop!"

They both started waving and shouting, but Ryker's ships were too far away and the wind too strong for their voices to carry.

"It's no use!" Elenna said as another cannonball whistled past. "We'll have to get closer."

Elenna tightened her grip on Sepron's scales as the serpent flicked his tail and struck off towards the distant ships. *BOOM* after *BOOM* rang out as the navy fired at the pirate ship. Elenna glanced back to see the flying vessel making for the shoreline where Verak waited, a blot of darkness beneath the stormy sky. Another missile arced towards Sanpao's ship. Elenna gasped as the cannonball slammed into the keel, smashing a hole. A gush of glowing purple liquid flowed out from the splintered wood.

"The ship's losing its flight elixir!" Elenna cried. The flying vessel lurched in the air, tipping sideways. Elenna saw a slender figure leap from the gunwale and land lightly on Verak's hunched form. *Ria!* A moment later, the ship careered

sidelong towards the ocean, crashing
down into the shallows beyond the
Beast. Elenna watched in dismay as
the main mast toppled and barrels

tumbled into the sea. *Amelia! I hope she's all right.*

Ria stood tall on the Beast's purple shell. Ignoring the wreckage of her own ship behind her, she lifted her long, glinting sword skywards. *Why doesn't the Beast throw her off?* Elenna wondered – then she remembered what Tom had said about the power of the sword.

More Avantian cannonballs plunged towards the beached pirate ship, punching great holes in the wood and ripping apart the sails.

Finally, Sepron drew up alongside the lead Avantian galleon and Elenna turned away from the wreckage behind them.

"Hold your fire!" Tom shouted.

Elenna could see Ryker at the helm, his chest puffed out further than ever.

"Hello, Elenna!" he cried, smiling down at them. "Cease fire!" he called to his crew, then he turned back to Tom and Elenna, practically glowing with pride. "We've done what we came for. Those ragamuffins didn't stand a chance against our superior cannons!"

"That may be," Tom said. "But we had a friend on board that ship." Elenna turned to see the pirate vessel half submerged, dark figures scrambling into the water and up the beach as the pirates started to flee. She swallowed hard, thinking of Amelia in among the chaos.

I hope she made it!

2

DISASTER AT SEA

"Let's get after those vermin before they escape!" Admiral Ryker called to Tom and Elenna. "We've got them right where we want them." Tom glanced towards the shoreline. Pirates fled the wreckage of the ship, scrambling into the shallows. Before them, Tom could see Ria standing tall on Verak's back, her expression fierce. He pointed.

"Sanpao's daughter commands that

huge lobster Beast. Your ships will be at its mercy if you get any closer. And in this storm, they are likely to run aground. Elenna and I will fight the Beast – you should retreat."

Ryker's face darkened. "Never! I swore an oath to King Hugo that I would protect Avantia's borders. It would be tantamount to treason to let such villains escape."

Tom felt frustration welling up inside him. Each gust of wind seemed stronger than the last and he could feel the force of the waves lifting Sepron's mighty body. The Avantian ships were in terrible danger.

"Admiral, with the greatest respect—"

"Look!" Ryker cut Tom off, shouting over the wind and the crash of the sea. "Out here on the waves my word is law and I say we should—"

A terrific gust tore Ryker's last words away. The gloom suddenly deepened. "Tom!" Elenna cried, pointing towards the shore. Horror gripped Tom's heart. Verak's bulbous claws beat the ocean, creating wave after wave, each higher than the last.

"Admiral, retreat!" Tom shouted, as the ships of the fleet started to rock. He could see Ryker giving orders to his crew but couldn't hear a word above the crash of the ocean. Sepron's massive body rose suddenly on the swell of a wave. Tom braced himself and tightened his grip... *Whoa!* His stomach dropped away, and the wave sucked Sepron down again. Before he

could catch his breath, the next wave
hit, even bigger. The sea crashed and
boomed against the hulls of Ryker's
vessels. Tom glanced shoreward and

his blood ran cold. A huge dark wall of water, higher than the spires of Irina's palace, rolled towards them.

"Turn about!" bellowed Ryker.

"Hang on tight!" Tom cried to Elenna.

Sepron turned to face the giant wave, and his serpent's voice filled Tom's head. *Hold your breath!*

"Elenna! We're going to dive," Tom cried, then took a gulp of air and flattened himself against the Beast's scaled back.

The thunderous roar of the sea filled Tom's senses – he could feel the vibration inside his chest. The wall of water was almost upon them – a churning, foaming, deadly force. Sepron lowered his head and dived. Tom clung to the Beast's neck ruff

as they plunged below the surface.
His stomach lurched and bubbles
swirled all around them. A powerful
current smashed them downwards
and water tugged and tore at Tom's
body. His lungs felt like they might
burst. Finally, the sucking, pulling and
churning lessened. The bubbles started
to clear. Sepron's powerful body angled
upwards, cutting through the water
so fast that Tom almost lost his grip.
They burst out above the surface, and
Tom took a grateful gulp of air. Elenna
gasped and coughed behind him. "Are
you all right?" he asked her.

"Just about," she answered weakly.
"But the fleet..." She trailed off, eyes
wide with shock.

Tom glanced about, and felt sick

with horror. The tidal wave had passed, but the slate-grey waters still heaved and crashed against what remained of Ryker's fleet. The ships leaned at crazy angles, the sails drenched and torn. Dark heads bobbed in the water where sailors had been swept overboard. Cries of alarm and hurried orders filled the air. Groups of sailors were already lowering dinghies into the sea.

Elenna clutched Tom's arm. "Verak!" she cried. Tom turned to see the vast Beast speeding through the water towards the stricken Avantian fleet, its yellow eyes blazing in the stormy light. Ria now stood on the lobster's broad back, her feet planted wide for balance, and her lips spread in an evil grin. The jewel in the hilt of her sword pulsed with light as she held it aloft.

"The sailors will have no chance! We have to distract the Beast!" Tom cried. He put his hand to the red jewel in his belt. *Are you ready for a fight?* he asked Sepron.

Always! the Good Beast hissed, though Tom heard a weariness close to exhaustion in his reply.

Waves churned and foamed around them as Sepron snaked towards Verak. The lobster's eyes seemed to spark with hungry glee as they fell on the mighty serpent. Ria lifted her sword, grinning wildly. Tom had his own blade raised ready to strike. As Verak drew within range, Elenna let an arrow fly. It pinged off the lobster's dark shell. Verak's huge claws swiped towards Sepron. Calling on the magical strength of his breastplate, Tom swung his blade with all his might. *CRASH!* Pain rang up his arm as blade hit shell, but the mighty claw recoiled. Sepron drew back, putting water between himself and the Evil Beast.

Verak rose up before them, his eyes blazing like pits of yellow fire. The ocean seemed to boil with rage, huge waves suddenly climbing in every direction, battering against them, almost sucking Tom from Sepron's back. Only Verak seemed unaffected, his huge dark bulk perfectly still in the whirling chaos. Thunder boomed overhead and lightning bleached the sky. Tom could hardly catch his breath. His arms and legs ached with trying to keep a grip on Sepron, who was struggling to stay afloat.

"Head for the shore," Tom told Sepron. "We can't beat this Beast at

sea."Tom tightened his grip on his sword as the Beast sliced through the roiling waves. As they drew close to the lobster, Ria shot Tom a cruel grin, her green eyes flashing with spite. She lifted her sword and swung a double-handed blow at Tom. He blocked with his shield but the force of the stab almost threw him from Sepron's back. Elenna grabbed his arm, stopping him from falling into the angry sea.

Tom felt a wash of relief as they sped onwards, leaving the lobster Beast behind. Sepron skimmed through towering breakers, then burst from the water up on to the beach, not far from the stone jetty. Tom and Elenna leapt from his back.

You must rest now, Tom told the

Beast. *Thank you for your help.*

Good luck, Tom! Sepron replied, then turned and, with a flick of his giant tail, vanished into the waves.

Tom scanned the ocean before him. The wreck of Sanpao's ship lay half-submerged in the shallows. Further out to sea, he could see the sinking ships of the Avantian navy, their masts poking from the water. And not far from the shore, eyes wild with hate, Verak stared back at him, as still and as massive as an island among the roiling waters. Ria stood on the Beast's back, a slender silhouette against the stormy sky.

I have to keep the Beast busy! I can't let it turn back to the fleet. Tom clambered up on to the stone jetty,

through arcing jets of spray, towards
the Beast. Foaming breakers crashed
around him, and his boots slipped
treacherously on wet seaweed. At the
end of the jetty, he stood tall in the
swirling, gusting wind and put his
hand to the red jewel at his belt.

Storm King! Tom called with his
mind. *I am Avantia's Master of the
Beasts. If you want a real fight, I am
the only person who can give you one.*

Verak's yellow eyes burned even
brighter. Thunder boomed overhead,
and forked lightning crackled across
the sky. The Beast's legs beat the
water and the colossal lobster surged
towards the shore.

Tom stood his ground, sword raised,
ready to meet the Beast.

THE BEAST'S FURY

"Kill him!" Ria shrieked from Verak's back. The Beast lunged, snapping out his two huge segmented claws. Tom threw up his sword and blocked, grunting with pain at the impact. He swung again, smashing his blade into the second claw, deflecting the blow. Ria leaned over and jabbed at Tom with the tip of her magical sword. Tom swung his shield, feeling

the force of the blow jolt up his arm
as he batted it aside. Already the
Beast's other pair of giant claws
reached towards him. Tom sent his
sword crashing into one, and angled
his shield to tackle the other. The
impact threw him backwards. His
heart lurched as his feet slipped
on the slimy stone. He caught his
balance just as Ria stabbed for his
throat. He leapt aside, swinging his
sword sideways and down, aiming
for Verak's bulbous, glowing eye.
The lobster recoiled and Tom's
blade struck the monster's club-like
forelimb, without leaving a mark.

"Ha!" Ria cried from Verak's back.
"You don't stand a chance! Your body
will be fish food! I'll— Argh!" An

arrow whizzed though the air and
struck the huge jewel in her sword,
sending the weapon spinning from

her hand. Ria's mouth hung open. Her eyes widened with fear. Elenna stepped to Tom's side, her bow in her hands and another arrow notched ready to fire.

"What's that you were saying?" Elenna called. The girl just stared back at them, gaping in shock.

"It's over!" Tom told her. "You can't control the Beast any more. You should give up while you still can!"

Ria blinked and shook her head, wringing her hands in dismay. "You think you've won, you idiots!" she cried. "But all you've done is set the Beast free. Now, no one controls him!"

As if woken from a dream, Verak suddenly bucked, throwing Ria high into the air. She landed in the sea and vanished in a perfect dive beneath the foaming waves. All four of Verak's crunching claws whipped towards Tom and Elenna at once.

"Run!" Tom cried. He turned on his heel and sped away with Elenna at his side. *CRUNCH!* The slick jetty shook as a mighty claw slammed into the stone behind him. Elenna stumbled and fell. Tom glanced back to see another pair of giant pincers striking their way. His heart in his mouth, he yanked Elenna to her feet, then tugged her into a run again, the Beast's claws crashing and crunching right behind them until, finally, they reached the beach and leapt down.

Tom turned to see Verak take one last vicious hack at the jetty, smashing chunks of stone into the sea. Then the creature reared up, its yellow eyes swivelling madly, and turned away, diving below the waves.

"What…now?" Elenna gasped at Tom's side. Further along the shoreline, Tom could see the last few pirates dragging themselves from the beached wreckage of their ship. In the deeper water, dinghies filled with Avantian sailors rowed frantically towards land, tossed like playthings by the waves.

"As long as we keep Verak's attention away from Ryker's men until they make it ashore, we'll best him eventually," Tom said, but his heart felt heavy and full of doubt. *If they make it ashore at all…*

Thunder cracked right overhead and lightning flickered across the sky. The wind howled and the waves rolled relentlessly towards them, smashing against the remains of the jetty. Tom spotted Ria in the water not far from the shore, swimming with exhausted strokes, though she hardly seemed to be moving at all. *She's caught in a riptide!* Tom realised. *I can't just let her drown.*

Tom ran down the beach and into the shallows, the waves sucking against his legs and slowing him down. He waded out deeper, avoiding the smooth water of the riptide, letting the rollers lift him up and carry him further until he could almost reach the struggling girl.

"Swim this way!" he called to her. Gasping, Ria spat out a mouthful of water, her head tipped right back and her eyes wide with fear. "Keep going!" Tom cried. Ria swam on, heading towards him. When at last she came within reach, Tom caught her arm and pulled her to him, out of the deadly current. She put her feet on the seabed, coughing and spluttering. Then she started to wade towards the shore.

"Are you all right?" Tom asked her as they staggered together through the shallows.

Ria turned and swung her fist. *Smack!* Tom's cheek exploded with pain. Somehow, he managed to keep his footing. He blinked away the water in his eyes to see Ria standing before him, her cat-o'-nine-tails crackling in one hand.

"We've still got a duel to fight!" she said.

FISH FOOD

Sanpao's legs felt heavy as lead as he staggered up to stand in the shallows. His muscles ached, but he was smiling. *Still alive!* He waded up on to the beach and sat down on the wet sand, gazing out to sea.

Huge dark clouds hung low over the raging ocean. Sanpao could see dinghies filled with Avantian sailors pitching wildly among the waves.

Ha! I love watching Avantians drown! Further up the beach, the remains of his own ship lay beached in the shallows, torn sails flapping crazily in the wind. Sanpao could see pirates crawling from the wreckage.

So, the backstabbing cowards survived! A faint twinge of guilt had tugged at Sanpao's gut when he'd left his daughter and crew to Verak – but not for long. *The treacherous, louse-ridden scurvy dogs left me for dead first...and Ria can fend for herself.*

Beyond the ship, huge waves crashed into the crumbling jetty. Two figures fought in the shallows alongside it – one with a crackling cat-o'-nine-tails. *That's my girl!* The other was an all-too-familiar boy with a sword. Sanpao let out a growl. *I should have known better than to think I'd got rid of Tom for good.*

Something glittering in the shallows caught his eye. Sanpao hesitated. *Well, if it isn't Ria's precious sword.* Last time he'd seen it, she'd been waving it at her new pet lobster Beast. Sanpao splashed over towards it, then pulled it from the sand. It felt weighty in his hands. He looked again at the huge gemstone, noticing the way it seemed to glow with a light of its own. *It's got to be worth a pretty sum. I think I'll take it for my troubles.*

Sanpao jabbed the tip of his knife under the edge of the stone. With a flick of the blade, the cool, heavy gem landed in his palm. Sanpao held it up, admiring its deep purple sheen, then he slipped it into his pocket.

Up the beach, Sanpao saw Ria and Tom still fighting. *Ria's got a knack with that whip*, he thought proudly as she lashed at Tom. *I'll leave her to it.*

Sanpao turned and headed away from the ocean, towards a clump of trees with dark shiny leaves. As he ducked into the thicket something heavy slammed into his back between his shoulder blades, pitching him forwards. He landed hard on his front, and the sword spun from his grip. Winded, and with the metallic taste of blood in his mouth, Sanpao scrambled to his feet and turned to face his attacker. He recognised the scowling face and fierce eyes of the girl from the ship. "You again!" *She must have dropped on me from a tree!* Sanpao stepped forwards to grab his sword from the ground, but before he could reach it, the girl snatched it up and sank into a fighting stance, frayed ropes still trailing from her wrists.

Sanpao lifted his hands, trying not to wince with pain. "Look, you crazy wildcat," he said, "you've got the loot, why don't you get lost and leave me

in peace?" *And with the jewel safely stashed in my pocket...*

"It's not the sword I wanted," the girl said, "it's you! I'm taking you back to Irina's palace!" But then her eyes suddenly filled with fear. She dropped the sword, whirled and ran.

Looks like she's seen sense, thought Sanpao, stooping to pick up the sword. He heard a loud shuffling sound, and froze. Then a hideous buzzing started up – like a swarm of bees inside his head. He spun round, and his guts turned to water. Verak loomed up, eyes burning with rage and huge, segmented pincers raised.

"Easy!" Sanpao said, lifting the magical sword as he'd seen his daughter do. "I'm your new master now. And it wouldn't do to eat your own master, would it?"

The monster before him paused, feelers twitching. Sanpao felt a huge wave of relief. But then a pair of massive claws swiped towards him, one pincer snapping shut about his waist. "Argh!" It hurt so badly Sanpao could hardly breathe. His mind flicked to the jewel in his pocket, and, through his pain and panic, he realised... *The sword doesn't work without the jewel in its hilt!*

A huge vertical slit, lined with rows of pointy teeth, opened beneath the Beast's hungry, glowing eyes. Terror gripped Sanpao. The useless sword slipped from his trembling fingers and clattered to the ground.

Time slowed to a hideous crawl and
Sanpao felt like his heart would burst
as the lobster lifted him up, bringing
him ever closer to its gaping maw…

SNAP!

Sanpao's mind went blank and
darkness closed over him as the Beast
swallowed him whole.

5

A DUEL WITHOUT HONOUR

Tom splashed through knee-high waves, dodging the sizzling arc of Ria's whip. The red-haired girl circled slowly, her eyes shining with spiteful glee. She let out a cackle of laugher and lashed at him again. Tom threw up his shield and felt the thud of nine sizzling tails strike it. The smell of singed wood filled his nose as he jabbed for Ria's gut with his sword. She brought her whip down on the blade, smacking it aside.

"Tom, I've got your back!" Elenna cried.

Ria smirked. "Oh! Does little Tommikins need his friends to help him?" she asked.

"I've got this!" Tom called back to Elenna. He scowled back at Ria. "You asked for a fair fight. That's what you'll get!"

But, as he fought on, ducking out of range of Ria's magical weapon, trying to get close enough to strike, frustration burned in his chest. Waves sucked at his feet, slowing his movements, and Ria's snaking whip forced him back. He almost toppled as something solid struck the back of his knees. He glanced over his shoulder to see that he had hit the edge of the splintered deck of Sanpao's ship. Tangled rigging and torn sails hung from the broken mast flapping in the gale. *Firm footing at last!* Tom vaulted up on to the listing deck. Ria followed.

Crack! Nine sizzling tails whipped towards Tom. He blocked with his shield, diving sideways towards the crooked mast. Grabbing the rigging, Tom swung upwards, climbing the ropes as fast as he could. Ria cracked her whip at him again. The fizzing tails almost caught Tom's leg, but he snatched it away, feeling a surge of hope as the weighted leather

whips tangled in the rigging. Tom saw
Ria's grin falter as she tried to tug
her weapon free. *It's stuck!* Seeing
his chance, Tom leapt, aiming both
booted feet at Ria's chest. *Boof!* She
flew backwards then rolled down the
deck, her whip tumbling after her. She

landed in the shallows with a splash. Tom leapt to her side and pressed the tip of his sword to her throat. Waves washed over the girl, making her cough and splutter.

"Yield!" Tom ordered.

"Never!" Ria snarled. More salt water slapped at her face, and she coughed.

"You don't have to do this!" Tom told her. "Just because your parents are evil doesn't mean you need to be. Instead of fighting against the kingdom, you could fight for it, like I do." Tom saw a flicker of emotion in Ria's green eyes – something like doubt. Her angry scowl seemed to soften. He lifted his sword just a little, so Ria could push herself up out of the waves.

"We can stop this now," Tom said.

Ria's face crumpled, and she started to cry. "You're…right…" she gasped, sniffling. "I don't want to be like Sanpao or Mama. I want to be normal. But it's so hard!" Ria hiccupped and choked.

Tom took a step back and lowered his sword. "Don't cry," he said, reaching a hand gingerly towards her. "We can help you."

Ria's booted foot shot out, and struck Tom hard in the shin. As he staggered back, she snatched her glowing whip from the water and leapt to her feet.

"Ready when you are!" Ria said cheerfully, brandishing her cat-o'-

nine-tails once more.

She's even more annoying than her parents!

A deafening crash rang out behind them. Tom looked back to see a giant purple claw clamped about the far side of Sanpao's ship. The claw gave a jerk, and the whole ship started to shake. Barrels and cannonballs rolled down the deck towards them.

Tom dived out of the way and crouched in the shelter of the quaking keel. Ria leapt to his side as the debris tumbled past. Her smile had gone once more, replaced by a wide-eyed look of fear. Tom peered out from their hiding place to see Verak heave himself over the gunwale and clamber on to the pirate ship. His

long feelers twitched and his eyes
swivelled about, glinting hungrily.
An arrow hit the Beast's shell and
clattered away. The Beast didn't even
flinch.

"I can't hold it back!" Elenna called

from further up the beach.

"We're both dead if we don't fight that thing together," Tom told the pirate girl at his side.

Ria bit her lip. Loud scraping, clacking sounds echoed down from above them. She took a deep breath. "So, what's the plan?" she said at last.

"Follow my lead," Tom told the girl. Then he stood and stepped out before the Beast. He half expected Ria to stay hidden, but from the corner of his eye he saw her step to his side. Verak let out a hiss of triumph as his glowing eyes fell on Tom.

"What now?" Ria said, her voice quivering with fear.

"If we attack together," Tom said, his eyes on the colossal purple monster before them, "we can win."

Verak's feelers whipped about in a frenzy as he clambered closer. The Beast's four pincers gaped wide, and a long, vertical mouth lined with jagged teeth opened beneath its glowing yellow eyes.

Tom swallowed hard, and lifted his sword. "Ready?" he asked Ria.

"Right behind you," she said.

Tom tightened his grip on his sword, his heart hammering as Verak bore down on them. A vast claw whipped out. At the same moment, Tom felt a pair of hands hit the base of his spine, catapulting him forwards. He tumbled, throwing up his arms to break his fall…

Before he hit the deck, Verak's pincer clamped shut about his middle and jerked him skywards. Tom spotted Ria's smiling face below him, just before he was tugged through the air in the grip of the Beast, and plunged headfirst into the raging sea.

6

FIGHTING EVIL

Cold horror washed through Elenna's veins as Tom disappeared below the waves, caught in the murderous grip of the Beast. Ria stood on the slanted deck of Sanpao's beached ship, her hands on her hips, gazing out at the storm-wracked sea. Elenna ran a few paces towards the shoreline. *I have to help Tom!* But she could already see the dark shape of the Beast streaking away from her through the water. *Taking Tom with him!* She shifted her gaze towards the horizon, and spotted what was left of the Avantian fleet. Unable to row against the vast waves, Admiral Ryker's dinghies had turned and were making for the tiny islands nearby – which meant they wouldn't be helping Tom either. A rush of hopelessness swept over Elenna. But then among the wreckage littering the sand at her feet, she spotted a cutlass. She lifted the weapon and weighed it in her hand. *I can teach that girl a lesson if nothing else*, she thought, as she charged over the sand towards Sanpao's ship.

"How could you?" Elenna screamed as she leapt up on to the deck behind

Ria and drew back her cutlass.

The pirate girl turned, smiling. "It was ridiculously easy, actually," she said. "That boy's such a trusting fool." Beyond her, the waves roiled. Verak's dark form burst up from the depths, and Elenna caught a glimpse of Tom

stabbing down at the huge pincer clamped around him, before Verak plunged him beneath the waves once more.

"He's a hero!" Elenna growled. "Something you will never understand."

"So, teach me," Ria said tauntingly, lashing with her weapon. Elenna leapt aside, and ducked behind the ship's broken main mast. As she peered out at the crackling nine-tailed whip, her throat tightened. The cutlass in her hand felt close to useless.

"Not so brave now!" Ria said.

"So, let's even the odds," a familiar voice shouted hoarsely. Amelia leaped up on to the deck. She looked soaked

to the skin, and exhausted. Frayed
ropes dangled from her wrists. But
her dark eyes glinted fiercely, and
she wielded a long silver sword. Ria
turned to face Amelia.

"My sword!" Ria cried. "What have

you done with the jewel?"

Amelia shrugged. "I'm guessing it's inside the Beast, along with Sanpao."

Elenna saw Ria stiffen. "Papa?" she said.

Amelia nodded. "The Beast swallowed him." For a moment, Ria's cat-o'-nine-tails hung loose in her hand. But then she straightened and lifted her weapon.

"I hope Verak's not allergic to scoundrel," Ria said. Then she pounced forwards, swinging her whip. Amelia swiped at the crackling leather strands with her sword, but let out a yelp of pain as the two weapons met, then scrambled away from Ria, clutching her arm. Ria tipped her head back and laughed, her feet planted wide and one hand gripping the rigging for balance. Elenna leapt from the cover of the mast and lunged for the evil girl, but at the same moment, the deck beneath her gave a shuddering lurch. Elenna's boots slipped on the soaked wood and she fell, landing heavily on her back, winded with pain.

Ria spun, sizzling whip raised and her eyes flashing. Elenna tried to struggle up, but the ship gave another lurch. Spray arced over the gunwale, soaking her through. Ominous creaks and groans rose from below decks and waves boomed against the hull. From the corner of her eye, Elenna saw Amelia charge towards Ria, but the ship tipped again, and she staggered sideways, slamming into one of the cannon.

Terror gripped Elenna's heart and squeezed as Ria swung her cat-o'-nine-tails back. The lengths of leather sizzled and crackled, and the sails from the broken mast flapped wildly above her. Seeing one last desperate chance, Elenna drew her arm back and sent her cutlass spinning through the air, up towards the sail's fastening. The blade sliced cleanly through a taut cord, severing it, and a huge section of heavy sailcloth crashed down over Ria, knocking her to the deck. Amelia leapt on top of Ria as the girl struggled beneath the folds of cloth. Elenna quickly joined her, pinning their enemy firmly.

"You're trapped," Amelia cried.
"Yield!"

A long, mirthless cackle of laugher
came from beneath the fallen sail.
"I'll never yield!" Ria cried. "You've
not seen the last of me!" The sailcloth

shifted as Ria lifted her arm. With a muffled bang and a flash of blue light, Elenna and Amelia toppled forwards, the sailcloth beneath them suddenly empty, a great hole singed in the fabric.

Amelia clambered to her feet, scowling. "I suppose she learned that trick from her mother!" she said.

"Along with how to be an evil, backstabbing villain," Elenna said, standing. As she gazed down at the hole burned in the sail, an acrid stench like the smell of spent gunpowder rose from the blackened cloth... *Of course!* Elenna felt a sudden rush of hope as an idea formed in her mind. She glanced out at the raging ocean, to see Verak

speeding through the waves – his
claw empty. Her heart gave a skip of
fear, but then she saw Tom crawl from
the waves and stagger for the beach.
He's still alive!

"I've got a plan to defeat the Beast,"
Elenna told Amelia. "But we'll have to
be quick! Tom needs us!"

A NEW MISTRESS

Tom waded towards the beach, gasping for breath. Chilled to the bone, he felt hardly any pain from his leg wound, but his sodden clothes made it hard to move. He knew he should hurry. Verak could burst from the ocean at any moment. But Tom had used all his strength in the fight to get free and make it ashore – and now he had nothing left – not even his sword and shield. He'd had to let them go, unable to swim with them weighing him down. *Maybe Sepron or Krabb will retrieve them after I'm gone*, he thought. His legs gave way and he sank to his knees.

Tom saw the colossal shape of the Beast rising from the waves. His gut clenched with fear. He looked desperately for a weapon, or anything that might help him survive this Quest. Sanpao's listing pirate ship bobbed and lurched further up the beach, swaying in the rising tide. Two slender figures stood on the deck. *Elenna and Amelia...they must see me – why don't they come?*

A vast, dark shadow fell over Tom and he heard the clatter of jointed limbs. He glanced back to see two giant pincers snapping his way. Calling on the magic of his golden chainmail for strength of heart, Tom dived and rolled. With a dull thud, the ground shuddered, and wet sand pelted against him. Turning his head, he saw Verak drawing a claw up from the sand, right where he had just been. The Beast's other huge double-clawed forelimb slammed down towards him. Tom rolled clear, then staggered up to hobble as fast as he could over the sand. But before he'd got even a few paces, the buzzing hum filled his mind. Tom gritted his teeth against the sound and stumbled on, but sickness rose in his throat and his legs folded. He crumbled into a ball, barely aware of anything but sickness, pain and the terrible sound.

It's over. I can't go on...

A pincer snapped shut about his waist and hoisted him up. He twisted weakly, thinking only of the Beast's toothy maw, ready to consume him.

BOOM! The Beast's terrible whining stopped abruptly, replaced by a bloodcurdling screech. Tom found himself falling through the air. He hit the sand and tried to roll, but the monster's giant pincer still held him tight. Tom looked over his shoulder to see Verak backing away from him – the claw that held him had been severed from the Beast's limb!

BOOM! A black missile whistled through the air and smashed a hole in Verak's purple shell. Tom glanced towards Sanpao's pirate ship to see Elenna standing beside a smoking cannon. *She's firing cannonballs from Sanpao's ship!* Tom realised. A rush of hope and gratitude lent him new

strength and he wrenched open the pincer clamped around his body.

Tom heaved himself up and turned to see Verak rear up on his jointed hind limbs. The Beast's feelers and remaining pincers lashed the air wildly. His yellow eyes rolled in a mad frenzy.

Beyond the Beast, Tom spotted a figure, charging over the beach, brandishing a long silver sword. *Amelia!* The girl drove the point of her blade deep into the Beast's hide with a furious scream. As steel met flesh, a flash of lightning blinded Tom. When he could see again, Amelia stood alone on the beach, the jewel-less sword clutched in her fist. Before her, a pile of muddy purplish sand marked where the Beast had been.

Verak's gone! We did it!

"Tom!" Elenna cried, running headlong over the beach. When she reached him, she threw her arms around him and squeezed. Amelia joined them, and for a long moment the three friends stood holding each other, victorious and relieved.

Finally, they broke apart, and Tom looked at the two soaked, grime-streaked girls, his heart swelling with gratitude. "Thank you!" he managed, his voice cracking. "Without you, I would be inside that Beast by now."

"Like Sanpao," Amelia said. "The Beast swallowed him – I saw it with my own eyes!"

Tom shuddered at the thought of

anyone – even a pirate – meeting the fate he'd so narrowly escaped.

Amelia crossed to the purplish remains of the Beast, and poked something with the toe of her boot. "Here's the jewel," she said, lifting a gleaming purple stone. "Sanpao had it in his pocket. And look!" She bent again, pointing at a half-buried orb. "The Pearl of Gwildor."

"The jewel is yours, Amelia," Irina's familiar voice said from behind them. Tom turned to see a bright portal edged with pale blue smoke before him. Irina and Freya stood side by side within it, smiling out at them. Tom's heart leapt with joy at the sight of his mother – pale, her head bandaged, but smiling. "You earned the jewel by slaying your first Beast," Irina went on. "And with it, you earn the title of Mistress of the Beasts."

Freya agreed. "You fought well," she said, "and now your apprenticeship with me is complete. I know of

another kingdom, not far away, which needs a champion of its own."

"Congratulations, Amelia!" Elenna cried. Amelia stood still and silent for a moment, staring at the jewel in her hand. Tom had an inkling he knew how she felt. Becoming a Master of the Beasts was a great honour, but a heavy burden as well.

"I know you'll be great," Tom told her. "You have the strength, courage and determination to serve your new kingdom well. But how did you know that sword would defeat the Beast?"

Amelia looked up at him, her eyes twinkling. "An educated guess," she said. "I've been studying your Quests. But I think I learned my most important lesson during our sparring session at the Palace."

Tom frowned, thinking back. Their practice fight seemed long ago, but, in reality, it was little more than a day. "What lesson was that?" Tom asked.

"Never to take your eye off the Quest, of course!" Amelia said, grinning. Tom smiled too.

"I've got some advice for you both," Elenna said. "What you need after a Quest is food, rest and a hot bath."

"Sounds good to me!" Amelia said.

"Me too!" Tom said, suddenly aware of his sore muscles. "And I'll rest easier knowing there are three Masters of the Beasts to protect the kingdoms from now on, not just two."

THE END

CONGRATULATIONS, YOU HAVE COMPLETED THIS QUEST!

At the end of each chapter you were awarded a special gold coin.
The QUEST in this book was worth an amazing 14 coins.

Look at the Beast Quest totem picture inside the back cover of this book to see how far you've come in your journey to become

MASTER OF THE BEASTS.

The more books you read, the more coins you will collect!

Do you want your own
Beast Quest Totem?
1. Cut out and collect the coin below
2. Go to the Beast Quest website
3. Download and print out your totem
4. Add your coin to the totem
www.beastquest.co.uk/totem

Look out for the next series of Beast Quest! Read on for a sneak peek at GRYMON THE BITING HORROR...

CHAPTER ONE

THE BROKEN TOMB

Tom gasped. The heavy lid of Tanner's stone tomb was cracked open.

"Who could have done this evil deed?" cried Captain Harkman, drawing his sword. "How could an enemy of Avantia enter this place?"

Tom strode forward, sliding his own sword from its sheath. "It must have been something powerful to have done so much damage," he said.

"A Beast?" ventured Elenna, running ahead of Tom, her bow in her hand, an arrow on the string. "Oh!" She stopped with a cry, staring at something beyond the tomb. "Oh, no!"

"What is it?" Tom rushed forward. His heart missed a beat as he saw the body that lay huddled on the ground on the far side of Tanner's tomb.

"Aduro!" he cried, recognising the elderly wizard at once. The old man lay motionless under his cloak.

Read GRYMON THE BITING HORROR to find out more!

Fight the Beasts,
Fear the Magic

Do you want to know more
about BEAST QUEST?
Then join our Quest Club!

Visit
www.beastquest.co.uk/club
and sign up today!

Are you a collector of the Beast Quest Cards?
Visit the website for further information.